FROM THE SAME A

Love Life
The Vampire's Tr

(The Peter Chronicles)
Happy Ever After
G.S.O.H Essential
A Fresh Start
PETER
All Good Things

9 Months Book One
9 Months Book Two
9 Months Book Three

Non-Fiction titles
im fine
PlentyOfFreaks
Wasting Stamps
Self-publishing: Releasing your book to the digital market

Short Story Collections
Scribblings From a Dark Place
Reviews, Critics & Mystery Shopping
The Story Collection: Volume One

Novellas
Smile
The Dead Don't Knock
Writer's Block
Buried
The Last Stop
The Chosen Routes
A Christmas to Remember (YOU choose the story)
Romance is Dead
The Breakdown

Picture Books
I Hate Fruit & Veg

Smile - Matt Shaw

© Matt Shaw

978-1-291-16673-6

The right of Matt Shaw to be identified as the author of this work has been asserted by him in accordance with the Copyright, Designs and Patents Act 1988.

All Rights Reserved. No part of this book may be reproduced or transmitted in any format without written consent from the publisher, except by a reviewer who wishes to quote brief passages in connection with a review written for insertion in a magazine, newspaper or broadcast.

The characters, and story, in this book are purely fictitious. Any likeness to persons living or dead is purely coincidental.

WITH THANKS TO:

Elena Helfrecht of Apokryphia Art

For the awesome job she did with the cover design and photography.

You can see more of her work at:

http://apokryphiaart.deviantart.com

http://apokryphiaart.jimbo.com

Or look her up on Facebook!

Introduction

I can't stop shaking. Most notably in my legs. Even crossing my right leg over my left and holding onto the knee with my hands, pulling it up a bit.... even that won't hide the shaking. If anything, it just makes it look worse as it makes my arms shake more noticeably.

Stupid.

Okay, just need something to distract myself.

Take my mind off it all.

Mobile phone.

Check my emails.

I released my shaking knee and reached into the trouser pocket on the right hand side of my boot-leg jeans. There's another missed call on it. Mum again. I can't talk to her. Not yet. Soon. I know I should. I just can't bring myself to tell her yet. The panic in her voice won't help the situation - nor will the blame she'll be sending my way. The telling off I'm to get. Hardly fair.

Is it really even my fault?

Of course it is. I'm the eldest. I'm the one who was supposed to be in charge. It's all my fault. Definitely won't call her back just yet. I don't need to be shouted at just yet.

They still might find him.

So much for checking my emails and distracting my fretful mind.

I slipped the phone back into my pocket.

Now probably isn't the best of times to be checking such trivial things as emails anyway. Not when he is out there somewhere - lost.

Should I be out there too? Looking for him?

No.

Smile - Matt Shaw

They told me to wait here, in this small security office. I don't know, maybe they're right... Part of me.... I just..... I just feel as though I should be out there, looking for him too. They put an announcement out for him, over the speaker system... feels like ages ago. Called out I was looking for him and he should make his way to the security office. Feels like ages ago. Surely he would have got here by now... probably eyes red raw from crying and shaking - scared I had abandoned him.

I stood up.

I should be out there. I should be looking.

What if he wasn't in an area where he could hear the announcement being made? Have they just made one announcement or do they warn other shoppers too? I told them what he was wearing - as best as I could remember - would they have called out for other shoppers to keep an eye out as well? Warned others that my brother was missing... would they bring him to the security office? Would he even go with them?

A couple more minutes. That's what I'll give them. A couple. No more. No less. After that, I'll go out there and look too. If he shows up here, they can always call me back too.

Jesus, I only turned my back for a minute. It was a minute! I swear! Turned back and he was gone. I looked around for him in the nearby toy shops thinking he would have made his own way there. A proper temper tantrum more or less as soon as we got to the shopping mall because I wouldn't take him straight to the toy shops. I tried to calm him down. I tried to tell him I'd take him after we had bought the shoes we were sent out for but he wasn't interested - didn't listen - just kept shouting and screaming... and tears. Not even real tears. The tears a young child does when they're trying to get attention... the tears a young child does when they're just trying to cause a scene.

I couldn't take him straight to the toys. He would have spent his pocket money and then wanted to go home and play with his new toys. I know he would. It's what I used to do when I was eight years old too. It would have made it even harder to get the school shoes mum sent us in to get. A pair for him and a new pair of shoes for me, for when I start college next week.

I glanced down to a shopping bag, on the floor, by my feet. His shoes. The box is so small. It just reminds me how small he is. And he's out there alone... CCTV monitors line the back wall of the security office... each screen filled with people milling around, getting on with their shopping and general

Smile - Matt Shaw

exploring. Each screen filled. And he's out there somewhere, amongst the hustle and bustle of it all. I need to be out there too.

Suddenly the door to the security office swung open and the head security officer came in. He wasn't smiling. Not the face of someone who had found the little lost boy.

"He hasn't shown up?" I asked, a small part of me hoping that the security guard was just playing a cruel trick in pretending my brother was missing still but, in reality, he was waiting outside the door ready to burst in shouting 'surprise'.

The security guard shook his head.

Mum's going to kill me.

SMILE

Smile - Matt Shaw

1.

Music blasted from the computer, across the room on my small office table - my favourite band; Muse. I find their music helps me zone out from the sounds and general disturbances of the family home - helps me concentrate on my writing - especially when my brother, Lewis, is kicking off.

Lewis kicking off - a frequent occurrence in this house. Normally over the silliest of things too. I never remember mum and dad being as soft on me as they are on him.

I guess it is true - the second child does have it easier.

I can't hear exactly what he is shouting about this time, I just get snippets of the tantrum between tracks when the computer goes quiet. I'm not even sure if mum or dad are trying to calm him down, or telling him off... or even in the same room as him! If they're talking to him they're either so quiet I can't hear them or his screaming is drowning them out. If that were me, I would have had a smack by now. Looking back at all of the tantrums I used to have, not that there were loads of them, I find myself cringing. I wonder, in years to come, whether Lewis will remember how he behaved and feel the shame I sometimes feel too.

Track change again, he's still screaming.

"Shut up!" I shouted.

Typical, now I've heard his wailing, my ears have honed in onto him and I can hear him over Muse. I lashed back, against the wall where I'm leaning, and banged on the wall. If he didn't hear me shouting for him to shut up - he might hear the banging - what with his room being directly next to mine. I hope he heard it; the thump hurt my hand a little. My bedroom door gently pushed open. I half expected Lewis to come in and give me a mouthful but it was mum.

"What's his problem this time?" I asked her.

Mum looked tired. Lewis often had a habit of wearing her down. She had to get up, most days, before six in the morning to make sure Lewis was ready for school. She'd drop him off before heading into the office, where she worked, for an eight hour day. By the time she got home, having collected Lewis from the 'After School Club' and made dinner... I guess she has plenty

Smile - Matt Shaw

of reason to look tired. I feel sorry for her. Maybe I'll drive him to school, and collect him, when I've passed my driving test in a couple of months.

Good reason for mum and dad to buy me a car, I reckon.

A conversation for another time.

"He wants to go to the shop," she sighed. She sat down on the end of the bed. "What's this song? I like it?" she asked referring to the music blasting from my computer.

I leaned across to a small control, next to where I laid on the bed, and turned it down.

"You look tired," I said.

Mum just smiled at me.

"Dad not here?"

"He's gone out," she said, "something at the office he needed to get finalized for a meeting next week. I don't suppose you want to take him to the shop, do you?" she continued.

"Lewis?"

"Just be nice to have a bit of peace and quiet whilst I get on with some house-work," she said.

"Why don't you just smack him? Let him cry his tantrum off..."

"You know why..."

Last year mum and dad took Lewis to the doctors when they couldn't get a handle on his mood swings. They just thought he was difficult until a friend of the family pointed out he may have suffered from ADHD.... attention deficit hyperactivity disorder, or something like that. From there on in.... it seems as though it gave him a green card to be a little shit. Mum and dad wouldn't possibly dream of smacking him - after all, the moods aren't his fault.... not really... just a chemical imbalance or some crap like that.

Maybe he needs a new course of medication.

Or a better therapist.

Smile - Matt Shaw

"It would really help me out," mum said. "You said you needed to get some new trainers for college..."

"I haven't been paid yet," not that I was expecting much pay from the part-time summer job I had, working in the local video store.

"I'll buy them for you..."

She must be desperate.

"You'll buy them?"

I can't remember the last time she bought me something - other than my birthday or at Christmas.

"I need to get some new school shoes for Lewis too," she said. "If you take him to the mall to find some shoes and get some for yourself... you could take him to the toy store afterwards. Let him spend his pocket money..."

Pocket money. I never used to get pocket money when I was growing up. Sure, I got cash but only after I had done some chores for it. Another perk of the ADHD? Seeing how they changed, after he was diagnosed... seeing how differently they started to treat him - I often wondered as to whether I should have tried to get myself diagnosed too.

"Please..." she said.

She did look tired. And to offer the bribe of the trainers, she must have been desperate for some 'alone' time.

"Fine.... but I don't want to get cheap trainers..." Just because she's tired, and I feel sorry for her, doesn't mean I shouldn't take advantage of the situation. "You going to give us a lift?"

"Bus fare?"

"In that mood?" we both stopped and listened to him still ranting and raving in the room next door. "Maybe you need to talk to someone... get his medication increased or changed."

Mum sighed as though I'd hit upon a much discussed topic of conversation, "Your father is taking him to Dr. Hood next week."

Smile - Matt Shaw

I could see in her eyes that mum had had enough. She was struggling with holding down the job, coping with Lewis' moods and keeping the house looking nice. I keep meaning to do more around the place for her.

I'll start tomorrow.

Until I go to college. I'll probably be busy after that.

"So about the lift?" I asked again in the hope she'd see my point about having to take him on the bus.

"You know he'll be okay once he knows he's going to the shops."

"Dad hasn't taken me out for a driving lesson this week...."

"He's busy, he'll make it up to you - he always does..."

"I've got the plates, you could take me."

"Please, can you just get the bus... please... for me?"

So much for the lift. Maybe I should just take a leaf out of Lewis' book and throw a massive strop. I look at mum and give it a little more, serious, consideration. If it works for him - it might work for me too... she looks tired. Really tired.

"I can't wait to get my license," I said, "fine.... we'll get the bus."

Mum smiled, "Thank you - I'll get your money.... and your brother."

She got up from the edge of the bed, and walked towards the doorway.

"Don't forget... I don't want cheap trainers!" I called out.

* * * * *

Standing at the bus stop - mum was right, Lewis' mood has improved. Sort of. He's not screaming anymore, on the plus side, but - instead - he's telling me what shops we're going into and which ones we're avoiding. Basically, he's being just as irritating as if he was still throwing a strop.

"And we're definitely not going into any clothes shops..." Lewis ordered.

Smile - Matt Shaw

I don't agree nor disagree with what he's saying. At the end of the day, we'll go to the shops I want to go to. We'll start with getting him his school shoes and then.... my trainers. After that, fair is fair, I'll take him to the toy shop which caused the initial tantrum back at home.

"What shops do you want to go to?" asked Lewis - after he finally finished listing the ones we definitely wouldn't be frequenting 'under any circumstances'.

I didn't answer him - no sense - he'll probably only kick off. I'm not sure whether mum even told him we had to get his school shoes today. I doubt it very much. If she had told him - would have taken longer for him to get out of the house. He would have just started complaining again... a quiet whinging sort of complaining which escalates up to yet another full-on tantrum. We all know how he works now.

"Alex.... Alex...... Alex.... Alex.... what shops?.... Alex.... Alex....."

"What?!" I snapped.

"What shops are we going to?"

"Shut up!"

"Alex..... Alex..... Alex........."

I love my brother. Sometimes. But it bothers me how he always gets what he wants. As though he's the Golden Child. Sure, I understand the imbalance in his brain... I understand what causes his moods... it just annoys me how mum and dad tip toe their way around him for fear of setting him off. More annoying was when they first found out about his condition - beforehand we used to go out, as a family, at least a couple of times a week... soon as they found out, though, we stopped going out.

It was 'easier' to wait for a film to be released on DVD than to bother seeing it at the cinema. It was 'easier' for mum to cook at home than to go to a nice restaurant for the evening. 'Easier' to buy a paddling pool, on a hot summer's day, than it was to have a family trip to the beach... everything was 'easier' if we stayed at home.

Sure, I was at the age where it wasn't 'cool' to be hanging out with your family but - I'd have liked to have made the choice myself, whether to hang around with them or not.... not have it forced upon me because of my fucked up brother and his moods.

Smile - Matt Shaw

"Alex.... Alex...."

"Be quiet and just wait for the bus," I said. Thinking about his many episodes is winding me up, probably best thinking about something else so we don't have a fall-out. Bus-driver probably wouldn't even let us on if we're having a full on shouting match at each other.

"I just want to know what shops we're going to visit..." he continued - like an annoying insect buzzing around your head whilst you're trying to sleep at night.

"Let's just get there, shall we...." I said in the hope it would be enough to quieten him. "Look, here comes the bus now."

I felt a little wave of relief wash through me, as the bus approached from up the road. So far so good and, better still, it's not too far into town before we're at the shopping mall either.

"What shops....." he continued.

I wonder whether it will be easier to walk.

Smile - Matt Shaw

2.

Suddenly the door to the security office swung open and the head security officer came in. He wasn't smiling. Not the face of someone who had found the little lost boy.

"He hasn't shown up?" I asked, a small part of me hoping that the security guard was just playing a cruel trick in pretending my brother was missing still but, in reality, he was waiting outside the door ready to burst in shouting 'surprise'.

The security guard shook his head.

Mum's going to kill me.

"We've just made another announcement over the speaker," said the security guard.

"I can't just stand here," I said. "I'll go and look for him too.... if he comes back - you can put a call out for me.... or.... or you can take my mobile number," I reached into my pocket and pulled my phone out again and instantly started to retrieve my number for the officer.

"It's best if you wait here. It would be best for him to see a friendly face, when he comes here... he's likely to be scared..." said the officer.

"Exactly. Scared. I'm not waiting here... please, take this number down," I said. I held my phone out for the guard. He simply shrugged and took it from my grasp before walking over to the desk. Taking a pen from the top drawer, along with a scrap of paper, he made a note of the number.

"We'll give you a ring," he said handing the phone back to me.

"Thank you." I slipped the phone back into my pocket.

"Just to let you know, though... the centre closes in an hour..."

"Well what happens then?" I asked.

The security officer didn't answer. He simply gave me, what he must have thought to be, a comforting smile. His smile offered no comfort. It's obvious

Smile - Matt Shaw

what happens in an hour - we find out whether Lewis wandered off and simply got lost... or whether he is no longer in the shopping centre.

"Is there anyone we can call for you?" the guard asked as I walked to the door, to begin my search.

I shook my head, "No thank you."

I'll look around for half an hour, I thought, *half an hour and then I'll give mum a ring.*

Part of me hoped I'd be able to find him in the half hour timeframe I'd given myself. That or he'd have made his way to the security office just as the announcement asked him. Either would be fine. Might even be able to bribe him with chocolates, or something, so as not to tell mum and dad.

Please show up.

Why did I have to be such a dick? Okay, don't think about that now. Concentrate on finding him. Where to start, though? Including the food hall, there's three floors here - not counting the car parking levels... no sense counting those... he wouldn't go down there. He knows I wouldn't be there. But then, maybe that's a reason for him to go down to those levels - because he knows I'm not there - the best way to get away from me.

Maybe he doesn't want to be found after our argument.

I told him I didn't want to see him.... maybe he's giving me what I wanted.

No, he's too stubborn for that.

He'd sooner just stand there and rant and rave instead.

He must be lost.

He has to be lost.

Okay, three floors then... would he go up to the food hall? Only a handful of fast food restaurants, pizza shops and a sandwich shop up there.... already eaten today....

Two floors then.

Rule the food hall out.

Smile - Matt Shaw

Where to start now?

Back to where I last saw him... the sports shop...

Good a place as any to start.

I hurried away from the security office, down the back corridor, towards the large double doors which led back to the inside of the shopping centre. As soon as I pushed one of the doors open, carefully so as not to catch anyone on the other side, I was swept away with the busy hustle and bustle of the crowds... hundreds of people frantically walking around trying to get their shopping done.

Funny, now I'm listening out to hear Lewis crying out - the general noise from the strangers seems louder than I'd noticed before. Their voices all blending into one to create a loud, unrecognizable din. If only there was a way to quieten all but Lewis down.

It's hard to break into a full-on run, because of the crowds, but I manage to gather enough speed to break into a jog. A hasty jog towards the escalators, up to floor two where the sports shop is. Trying to think like a lost, eight year old boy.... this place must feel enormous to him. So many shops. So many people. So many unfamiliar faces coming out of nowhere... so much noise. He must be petrified. If I were his age and in his position, I would have been. Especially in this shopping centre - one of the biggest. Perhaps asking him to make his way to the security office was a bad idea. Would he know where it is? I had to ask someone.... would he even ask?

Surely, he would... he's not stupid. Difficult - yes. Stupid - no. But then, he's lost. Probably not thinking straight. Probably panicking. I hope I find him in the sports shop. I hope.

It would be great if he was there. Sat on one of the many chairs that lined the wall, next to the trainer display.... sat there acting all innocent, as though he had never wandered off in the first place. If I do find him - I won't shout at him for running off. I'll just be grateful that I'd found him....

If I find him?

When.

When I find him.

Definitely no shouting.

Smile - Matt Shaw

Stuck behind some fat people, on the escalators now. No point trying to say 'excuse me' - even if they both moved to the side, on their own step, there still wouldn't be room enough for me to squeeze by. On their way to floor three, no doubt.... the food hall. I dodge past them as soon as we all step off the escalator... okay, I can see the sports shop now. Over by Julian Graves, the health store.

As I get closer to the store, I can see through the window that it's not as busy as earlier... the staff members milling around by the till-point, no doubt counting down the minutes until the shop closes - thirty minutes before the centre does. Everyone seems to be relaxed and having a laugh - can't see anyone making a fuss over a little, lost, eight year old boy.... Keep optimistic... it doesn't mean he isn't in there...

Running now.

I run through the main entrance and straight over to the trainers. To the store staff, I must just look desperate for a new pair of runners as one of them approaches me almost immediately.

"Good afternoon, can I help you with anything?" asked the blonde shop assistant. Either keen at greeting customers or keen to get me to leave so they stand a chance of getting out on time. I'll never know.

"My brother...." out of breath.

How embarrassing. I thought I was fitter.

"Excuse me?"

"My brother.... I was in here earlier and he wandered off.... has my brother been in here looking for me? He's eight and he's lost...." I sound like I'm out of breath and panicking... I *am* panicking. I *am* out of breath.

The shop assistant shook her head, "I'm sorry," she said, "I haven't seen anyone like that... not anyone who wasn't with a parent anyway.... we do get children in here..."

What if he was with someone?

He wouldn't have looked lost.

A photo - need a photo.... phone... I've got a picture. Once more, I fished in my pocket for my mobile phone. Upon pulling it out I navigated through to the pictures and found one I had taken of Lewis when he was in a full-on strop...

Smile - Matt Shaw

something to embarrass him with when he was older... Not the best of pictures but better than nothing.

"Him... have you seen him? He's my brother and he's lost," I repeated. Still out of breath. Still panicking. Mum's going to kill me.

Again, the shop assistant shook her head, "I'm sorry...."

I dropped down onto one of the chairs. Shit. I really hoped he would have been here - or, at the very least, they would have seen him and helped him to the security office. Now what.... now where....

The girl gave me a sympathetic smile, "Well, I hope you find him... maybe you should ask them to put a call out...."

"They have already," I said, deflated. She stood, for a moment, looking a little awkward - unsure of what to say to try and make me feel better - before she about-turned and walked away leaving me to my misery.

Now what...

The toy store, I had checked earlier when I realised he was missing but... maybe he had only just left my side and I got to the shop before him - I did, after all, run as fast as I could. It would have been quite easy for me to run past him without spotting him amongst the crowds.

Why didn't I think of that earlier - perhaps I should have walked to the toy shop... or, at the very least, waited enough time there on the off-chance he had shown up a couple of minutes later. Instead I had run there, seen he wasn't there and then ran onto the security office without really thinking.

It's fine to run now though, I think as I start to pick up speed. It's easier to run faster now too - what with the majority of the shoppers making their way back to the mall's exits and car park floors. Still enough people milling around to make it hard to spot Lewis, though.

Please be at the toy store.

Please.

I'll never be horrible to you again.

As I dodge around the happy shoppers, I apologise for knocking into a few of them. I'm sure they'd understand my rush if they knew the circumstances.

Smile - Matt Shaw

Thankfully it's not too far to run - the toy shop Lewis likes is on the same floor as the sports shop I was trying to get my trainers in.

Hang a left out of the sports shop, run past Julian Graves, a few ladies' clothes shops, the computer game shop, the bookstore, a small fountain which is stuck randomly in the middle of the walkway.... past a few other clothes stores and the chemist and you're there.... the toy store.

Strategic placing - having the toy store next to the chemist. Mothers are always needing to pop to the chemist for bits and bobs - or even to treat themselves from the chemist's large perfume counter, of all things. I wonder how many of them have kids who spot the toy store.

Growing up I remember what I was like, with mum, when I spotted a shop I wanted to go into. I'd make such a fuss about going into it, mum would often say 'okay' and we'd go in.

"But I don't have any money," she'd always say.

Yet, nine times out of ten - I still left with some sort of present... even if it was only a toy yo-yo or a new, squishy ball from the cheaper back area of the store... I'd normally get something.

Casting my mind back to how I got when I saw a shop I wanted to go into - I should have just taken Lewis first. Taken him to the shop. He could have bought himself a toy with his pocket money and then, when we were looking around for my trainers, he could have kept himself occupied with whatever he bought. I should have done it that way round.

I'm an idiot.

In the toy shop now and it's nearly empty. A few people in here, looking at various toys... plastic action figures, toy guns, one child choosing a new doll to add to, I guess, a pre-existing collection.... her mother telling her to hurry up because the store is closing soon... A few people in here but not Lewis.

I pulled the phone from my pocket and approached the counter - at least I know Lewis would have been in here. Maybe the young girl behind the counter had spoken to him, maybe even got her manager to take him to the security office..... but then, I would have had a call from them.... full signal and no missed calls, other than my mum's missed call earlier.

"Excuse me," I said, "I was wondering whether you've seen my brother..."

Smile - Matt Shaw

I didn't wait for her to answer, I simply held up the mobile phone showing the same picture I showed the assistant in the other shop. She looked at it and shook her head.

"I don't think so.... but my colleague might have," she said.

"Is she around? Can you ask?"

Again, she shook her head, "Her shift finished about an hour ago... she won't be back until tomorrow now."

That doesn't mean she didn't see him, though. Without her being able to say one way or the other - it doesn't mean he wasn't here. He could have still made his way to the shop, by himself.

I want to believe that... I need to.

If he hadn't been here.... if this woman could say for definite Lewis hadn't been here.... well, that would be worse...

This still leaves hope, though.

He could still have made it here...

I'd rather think that then think of him not coming....

.... if he hasn't been here... hasn't made it to the shop he was desperate to come...

... well, he might have been taken.

No, don't think like that.

There's no definite answer as to whether he came here.

Of course he came here.

He wouldn't have been taken.

No.

No way.

Had someone grabbed him - he would have screamed the place down.

Smile - Matt Shaw

Besides, he was in a foul mood by the time he left... who would have wanted to take him?!

That's cruel.

He's lovely.

He's my brother.

He's.....

.... missing.

I need to phone home. Need to let mum know.

"Are you alright? Did you need to call anyone?" asked the lady behind the counter - a genuine look of concern on her face. I smiled at her. No point dragging her day down too.

"It's fine," I said, "he's probably already at the security office.... they put a call out for him already."

The lady smiled, "I must have missed it... Well, if he shows up - I'll call through to the office... can I see the picture again to refresh my memory?"

I showed her the photograph again and thanked her.

The shops are closing now. Soon the place will be empty, just before the doors are locked. I can't put the phone call off anymore.

Need to phone mum.

She's going to kill me.

Smile - Matt Shaw

3.

I stepped back into the security office only to be confronted by the sight of two officers playing with a deck of cards. Laughing, with cups of coffee in front of them, they seem happy. I'm glad for them.

"Did my brother show up?" I asked, ever hopeful.

"Not yet," said a guard from the other side of the room. His abrupt tone made me jump, I hadn't seen him there, tucked away, when I first walked in. Like the other two guards, he didn't seem to be too worried about finding Lewis either - just sitting on a chair, a newspaper in his lap and a mug of coffee to his side.

"I showed you guys the photograph," I said. "Shouldn't you be out there looking for him?"

The guard in the corner of the room, I presumed to be the man in charge, folded his newspaper up and turned his attentions to me - perhaps suddenly realising I might log a formal complaint against him if he didn't at least appear to be interested, "We've made announcements... we have a couple of guys out there looking for him... we've been monitoring the monitors... what else are we supposed to do?"

"I don't know," I said. I felt my face redden with embarrassment. This is all my fault and yet I'm expecting these strangers to set things right for me again. My dad always told me you tidy up your own mistakes.

"Not long before the shopping centre closes... it should be easy to see him when everyone else has left," the guard continued. The other guards didn't say anything - just kept staring at the deck of cards in their hands.

"And what if he leaves with everyone else?" I asked. I could just envision Lewis now - wondering the streets looking for me... panicking... A horrible thought. Alone out there. And the feeling of loneliness is normally multiplied when you're surrounded by crowds, for some strange reason. The security guard didn't have an answer for me. "Should we call the police?" I continued.

The two guards on the other side of the room, next to the monitors, stopped playing cards and turned to face me, "Do you really think we should disturb the police at the moment?" one of them asked.

Smile - Matt Shaw

"My brother is missing..."

"For all of about an hour or so," the second card playing guard said. "Missing children need to be reported after twenty-four hours.... you know.... he could still show up. He could still walk through the door, any minute now, clutching a bag of toys in his hand... you did say he wanted to go and spend his pocket money... maybe that's what he is doing... Look, why don't you take a seat, have a hot drink and wait until the store closes..."

"A hot drink? Should I be playing cards too? My brother is missing... for all you know he could have been taken... but you're still happy to sit there playing cards... How did you get your jobs?!"

"And for all you know - he's fine and just hiding from you. To teach you a lesson for being horrible to him... you did say you were being horrible to him, right? As my colleague said - just wait a bit longer. The mall will be shut, we can give the place a final sweep - all of us... chances are he'll turn up..."

I felt as though two of the three guards were ganging up on me. They couldn't care less that Lewis was missing. At least, that's the impression they gave. The third of the guards was staying relatively quiet. "What about you?" I asked the quieter of the guards, "what do you think?"

He simply shrugged, "This is my first week," he said, "I haven't been involved in anything like this yet.... but my colleagues...."

The lonesome guard in the corner butted in, "... but his colleagues see this quite a lot and know how many children show up... Trust us."

"And of all the kids who do show up - how many fail to come back?"

The guard didn't say anything.

"I have to call my mum," I said.

I stepped out of the main office, back into the deserted hallway, to phone home. I didn't need the security guards hearing this conversation. Not with the way they were being. Mind you, if I played the reaction through the loud speaker of the phone and they heard how upset mum will be.... I wonder if they'd suddenly feel more compassion.

I selected my home number, via the contacts list of my phone, and pressed the green button. Seconds later and the call connected - the ringing tone playing through the ear-piece at me.

Smile - Matt Shaw

I wish Lewis had shown up. I didn't want to be making this call. Mum, and dad for that matter, know what Lewis is like. They both know what a handful he can be. They've both experienced it for themselves... even so, I bet this is going to be my fault.

It is my fault. I can't pretend otherwise.

The phone clicked, on the other end of the line, and I heard mum's voice, "Hello?" She sounded as though I'd just woken her up. Great.

"Mum, it's me," I said.

"Oh, hi, how you getting on? You on your way home soon?" she said - missing the sheepish tone of my voice.

I wasn't sure how to break this news to her. How to say Lewis has run off without sending her into a complete panic. How to say you've lost your brother without then getting an ear-bashing as the news slowly sinks in. How to say I don't know where he is. Security guards don't know, or care, where he is... no one knows... he's lost. How do you tell someone that?

"Can you hear me? Are you there?" she continued.

I'm going to have to tell her something, break it to her as gently as I can, "Mum, Lewis isn't with me... he's run off..."

There was silence. A quick check of the mobile phone screen reveals a full service is available.

"What? Well, where is he?"

She sounds worried.

Not angry.

Worried.

"I don't know, mum, they've been making announcements over the speaker system for him but he hasn't shown up yet.... Mum, the mall closes soon, I think you need to come down here..."

"I'm on my way."

Smile - Matt Shaw

"Just come to the security office," I said. "I'll meet you there, I'm going to go and see if I can find him again."

"Just wait at the office! I don't need to lose both of you!" she snapped.

Great, now she sounds angry.

"How could you let this happen?"

She didn't wait for an answer. The phone line went dead.

I slipped the phone back into my trouser pocket. I should have stayed at home, on my bed, writing.

* * * * *

Holding Lewis' hand, so he didn't run off like he normally did when we went shopping, I pulled him in the direction of the first shoe shop I saw.

"Where are we going?" he yelled - same loud volume he usually used when he sensed things weren't going in a direction he approved of, "The toy shop isn't in this direction!"

"We aren't going there, yet." I said. I hoped he understood the word 'yet'. "Mum told me to find you some school shoes first.... school shoes first and then the toy shop."

"But I want to go to the toy shop... that was the whole point in coming!" he was starting to try and pull away from me so I simply tightened my grip.

"And we will be going there, but after we've got you some school shoes!"

"I don't want to go and get school shoes! I don't need school shoes! I don't like them!" he started to get louder.

I stopped pulling him and turned around to face him - dropping to his level, in the process. I whispered, "Mum wants you to have some new school shoes for when you go back.... look.... you're going to have to get them. But, with me, you can choose anything... any pair you want... even if you think mum will hate them! You can get them! Otherwise, you'll have to come back here with mum and you'll end up getting a pair that she likes...."

Smile - Matt Shaw

Lewis didn't say anything. I could see from his expression, though, that he understood what I was saying... with his cool brother, he gets to choose any pair he wanted - maybe even the pair that offered the free 'lightening strike' badge like his friend had last year... Or the shoes with the flashing lights built into the heals...

"Sooner we've got your shoes," I continued, "the sooner we get to the toys! Deal?"

I hoped he agreed but tried not to show my desperation. I wasn't in the mood to fight my way around the shopping centre with him. I couldn't be bothered with it all. I just wanted a new pair of trainers. Lewis hesitated for a moment before nodding, "Deal."

I breathed a sigh of relief.

"Okay, this way," still holding his hand, I pulled him in the direction of the shoe shop. Get his shoes first, then my trainers and then, if there's time, a quick trip to the toy store so he could spend his pocket money. The less I spend on his shoes, the more I get to spend on my trainers.

"You don't have to hold my hand!" he barked from a few paces behind me. I slowed down to allow him the chance to catch up a little bit. I forget I have longer legs. Harder for him to catch up when I hit my stride. "I won't run off," he said.

"I don't want you getting lost in the crowd," I said, not letting go of his hand. Of all the days to come to the shopping mall, I think we'd chosen the busiest. God only knows what the queues are going to be like, inside the actual shops. I hate queues. Especially when I have Lewis with me - the ticking temper time-bomb. He gave another little struggle, against my grip, but I didn't loosen it until we crossed into the first shoe shop. "Go and have a look around," I told him. He didn't need any more permission before he ran off towards the children's shoes - against the far wall of the shop.

I left him to it for a while, so as not to cramp 'his style', and browsed the shoes in the men's department. They all look the same....

Plain...

Simple...

Boring...

Safe...

Smile - Matt Shaw

The sort of shoe you'd choose to wear, I hazard a guess, if you were sat at a desk for the majority of your working day. They look the part but probably couldn't take much wear and tear before they started to look as though they were ready to fall off your feet, in pieces. For the price, though, what did people expect.

Probably the cheapest shoes I've ever seen.

I remember why I'm in the store - looking for school shoes for Lewis. Cheap is good. It's not like I'll be getting my trainers from here, after all. Just need to convince him to like a pair in here, as opposed to one of the more expensive shops further into the mall... and I know the perfect way to convince him... I walked over to where he was looking at the trainers.

"You're looking for shoes," I reminded him.

"These are shoes!"

I frowned, "You know what I mean..." I pointed in the direction of the black shoes, a few shelves away from the trainers he was looking at.

"I don't like them!" he said.

"No one likes school shoes," I said. "You just need to choose a pair and then we can go... the sooner you choose them.... the sooner we get to the toy shop! Right?"

"I don't want to choose a pair!"

"Grab any pair just to keep mum happy or you'll have to come back with her and she'll drag you around *all* of the stores to find a pair she likes... I mean, if you'd rather that and spend a whole day trying on different shoes... that's cool..." I picked up a pair of the cheapest looking shoes... "Look, these are nice..."

"No, they're not!"

"Well, no, they're not... but we could buy them and then.... it's done. No more shoe shopping! Straight to the toy shop!" after I'd chosen some trainers, that is. No need to tell him that yet. Just get this bit finished first. If he's being difficult now, he'll only get more troublesome when he realises we have other shops to visit before he gets to the shop he really wants to go to. "You don't even have to try them on... what do you think?"

Smile - Matt Shaw

Lewis was on the verge, I'm sure, of saying 'yes' when the shop assistant approached - a larger girl who looked as though she really wanted to be somewhere else. "Did you find what you were looking for?" she asked.

I turned to Lewis, "What size are you?"

He simply shrugged, "I don't know..."

"Can we get his feet measured?" I asked the assistant.

She rolled her eyes and disappeared to the far wall, where she collected the necessary equipment to measure Lewis' feet - a piece of wood with a sliding scale on it.

"You said I don't have to try anything on," moaned Lewis.

"You don't," I said. "I just need to measure your feet and then we're done. That's it! Promise."

Lewis gave me what he thought to be an Evil Look but I paid him no attention and he begrudgingly kicked his shoes off, before putting his left foot onto the contraption which was now on the floor in front of him - the large girl kneeling in front of him.

She slid the top bar down the bar until it touched the top of Lewis' foot, "Size six..." Lewis stepped off and she beckoned him to put his right foot onto the board. Again, she slid the top bar down to the top of his foot, "Just over a six..."

"Okay," I said, "let's call it size six then." I turned back to Lewis and held up the cheap shoe I found, "What do you think?"

"No more shoe shops?"

"For you," I said. Not a lie. The other shoe shops will be for me. Lewis nodded towards the shoe - closest I'll get to an approval, I handed it to the shop assistant who took it and disappeared out the back - no doubt to find the other shoe. I wonder, at that price, does it come with a box too?

Minutes later and we were at the till point - Lewis was chomping at the bit to get out of there but I told him to be patient. After all, wouldn't take long to ring it through the till. This shop is all about selling the most amount of shoes in a day - this girl wouldn't want to be stuck serving us. Especially as the shoes are not even ten pounds. She'll want to be back on the shop floor trying to hit her target to avoid a ticking off at the end of the day.

Smile - Matt Shaw

Not even a tenner.

They won't be comfortable.

What do I care?

I won't be wearing them.

Lewis is really going to suffer when he's wearing them all day at school.

Did I really just snigger at the thought of that?!

Cash handed over.

Shoes boxed and bagged.

Receipt and change passed back.

Job done. Job done and that bargain shopping meant I had sixty-three pounds left to spend on my pair of trainers. Well, I did tell mum I wasn't going to get a cheap pair...

As I left the shop, I felt an unexpected pang of guilt shoot through me. She had given me seventy pounds to spend on a pair of trainers, a pair of shoes for Lewis and a drink and cake each from the mall's cafe. I decided we didn't need the drink and cake and.... well... she never specified how much I was to spend on each pair of shoes. I'm sure Lewis' shoes won't be that bad... He might just have to break them in for a month or two.

Maybe three.

Smile - Matt Shaw

4.

Mum was looking at the shoes Lewis and I chose, for him to wear to school, in the security office. Her eyes were watery, as though she'd been crying before she got there. Two of the security guards had left the office to look around and close various bits of the shopping mall - leaving the quieter of the guards with us.

"Have you ever had abductions from this shopping mall?" she asked the security guard, finally breaking the awkward silence.

"He's new," I told her.

She flashed me a look as if to say 'be quiet' - like she wanted the guard to answer for himself.

Taking note of the look mum flashed me, he answered, "Your son's right. I'm new here... but I understand that children go missing quite a lot but they tend to show up..." He smiled at mum, a smile of reassurance.

She didn't smile back.

"So where is he then?" she asked. The security officer didn't answer so mum turned to me, "Well? Where is he? Where's my son? Where's your brother?"

I looked to the floor, I couldn't take looking her in the eyes which flashed from worry to anger to disappointment. Worried about Lewis. Angry at me for losing him. Disappointed in me for not being a better brother. A better son. A reliable son. Is this really in her eyes or am I just making it all up.

"Well?" she wanted an answer.

"I don't know," I said. "I've been looking for him. I've looked everywhere."

"And what have you done?" she asked the guard. The guard, like me, struggled to look mum in the eye.

"We've been making announcements..."

"He's eight years old. Do you really think he's been listening out for your announcements or do you think he's been lost in his own world of worry?"

Smile - Matt Shaw

Mum had a point. Would I have heard announcements being made for me if I were his age and lost? The security guard didn't answer.

"Have the police been called?" she continued.

I didn't answer. I learnt my lesson from the earlier look she shot me.

"No," said the guard.

"And why not? Don't you think it would be a smart move?"

"My colleagues said they wouldn't come.... it's not been long enough..."

"He's eight years old and he's by himself! How long is 'long enough' exactly?"

"Mum, he's new..." I was starting to feel sorry for the security guard. I understood mum was worrying and upset but, this bloke really wasn't the one to answer her questions. The other security guard should have stuck around to answer the queries. He's had more dealing with me today, and knows more about other cases of missing children. He should have sent the newer guard around with the other man... it was almost as though he wanted to get away from the questions.

"Then who's in charge?" she asked. "I want to speak to the person in charge! Where's the management?"

The security guard took his window of opportunity to escape, "I'll find him...." He stood up and left me with my mum.

No sooner had the door closed, mum broke down into floods of tears. I crossed the room and put my arm around her. I knew it wouldn't make anything better. I knew it wouldn't fix anything. I just hoped.... I just hoped it'd offer her some sort of comfort.

She pushed me away, "How could you let him run off? You knew what he was like... you know... how could you?" The tears are still flowing but she's angry again. Her emotions bouncing all over the place.

"I didn't mean to! I turned my back for a split second... a second," I said - not quite shouting but not exactly speaking softly either. I knew I had done wrong. I knew I had caused this but I felt enough guilt as it was. I didn't need her shouting at me. No matter how much I deserved it.

"What happened? Why did he run off?" she asked - calming ever so slightly.

Smile - Matt Shaw

I'm still not sure he did run off.

Had he run off - surely he would have surfaced by now... probably with a new toy, bought with his pocket money...

If he had run off....

.... he would have heard the announcements...

It's been in my mind since he's been missing but....

...what if....

...what if he didn't run.

What if he was snatched?

I've been wanting to ignore it but... where is he?

He should have appeared by now.

What if he was snatched?!

How do we get him back?

How do we find him?!

What if we don't find him?

What if he's gone now?

"Please, tell me, what happened," she repeated.

I can't tell mum what I'm thinking.

Chances are, she could well be thinking it herself but... she doesn't need me saying it too.

Saying it out loud...

It makes it all the more real.

"Did you see him speaking to anyone... at any stage?" she asked. "What happened... what made him go?!" her voice was getting more frantic.

Smile - Matt Shaw

"It was after we got the school shoes..." I mumbled - I already know she's going to be even angrier with me when I tell him I didn't take him directly to the toy store, as I had promised him. I knew it would only wind him up. Maybe, deep down, I wanted to upset him. Not sure.

I never wanted him to run off, though.

* * * * *

"You're going the wrong way!" Lewis protested after we left the shoe shop, having just purchased the cheapest pair of shoes I'd ever seen.

"I just need to get some trainers," I said in a very matter of fact tone - more or less dragging him by his spare hand. His other hand clutching onto the bag of shoes.

"What? You said there'd be no more shoe shops..."

"No, I said you wouldn't need to try any on...." I replied although, technically, he was right of course.

"What about the toy shop?"

Lewis and that damned toy shop. I know, though, he'll be itching to get home after going to the store. Itching to get home to play with whatever tat he's got his heart set on this time - whether it's the latest action figure, a new piece of lego or this water-pistol he keeps seeing advertised on the television. Although, why he'd want that I don't understand... surely to get the most from a water-pistol, you need friends to play with and he rarely leaves the house - let alone ventures off with like-minded pals.

"We'll get to the toy shop, I just need to get myself some trainers first and then we have the rest of the afternoon...." not that there's much of the afternoon left. Maybe it would be easier to keep the money and come back tomorrow, without Lewis. Mind you, mum would probably insist on me taking him again - just so she can have a bit more time to herself. No. I'll get it done now. It won't kill him to wait a while longer.

"We could go to my shop first and then go to your shop...." he continued.

Nice try.

Smile - Matt Shaw

"We've already been to one of your shops," I said, "it's my turn now." A cruel way of looking at it but fair is fair, after all.

"Mum said you had to take me to the toy shop!"

"Mum told me to get you out of her hair because you were doing her head in," I corrected him. "Just like you're doing my head in now.... now shut up - we're going to get the trainers and then I'm taking you to your fucking toy shop!" I shouldn't have sworn... hopefully he didn't hear....

"I'll tell mum you swore."

He heard.

"And I'll beat your head in," I said. The threat of violence from an older brother was normally enough to quieten any threat of snitching to the parents. I noticed my shoelace was undone and stopped - momentarily letting go of his hand so I could tie it back up.

When I had completed the knot, I glanced over to Lewis who had gone quiet. He was stood next to me staring at a clown who was making a sad face back at him.

I hate clowns.

Always have.

I place the blame with Stephen King.

Still, it was nice to see Lewis quiet. He didn't know what to make of the clown who was starting to rub his eyes, as though he were pretending to cry. He suddenly stopped with both of his hands covering his face...

"BOO!" the clown suddenly shouted as he took his hands away to reveal the most manic smile I've ever seen. Was this supposed to make Lewis smile or scare the shit out of him? Lewis didn't bat an eye-lid and slowly the clown's smile turned back into a sad face. Seconds later the clown, dressed in a yellow and red outfit with a massive red and white spotted bow-tie and overly large red shoes, mimed having an idea.... as though a lightbulb went off in his head. He raised a finger, "Ah HA!" Lewis just kept on looking at him - mesmerized by the sheer craziness. The clown reached into a pocket, on the side of his pocket, and pulled out a handkerchief.... a handkerchief which appeared to be attached to numerous other handkerchiefs.... the more he pulled, the more came from his pocket.

Smile - Matt Shaw

By now a crowd had gathered to watch the clown trying to entertain Lewis. Some of the other children were laughing and enjoying the antics but Lewis just kept looking at him as though he were not from this planet. Who knows - maybe he is right. Maybe they aren't. Would certainly explain the general creepiness about them.

Finally the handkerchiefs ran out and the clown dropped them to the floor, smiling his manic smile once more. He fished back in his pocket and pulled out a red balloon. I already know what's coming. Sure enough, the clown started to blow into the deflated balloon - slowly inflating it. As soon as it had enough air in, the clown tied a knot in the balloon's neck.... fishing back in his pocket he pulled out a piece of string and effortlessly managed to get that around the balloon too... I have to confess, I was expecting a balloon animal not 'just a balloon'.... a balloon with the word 'smile' written across it in thick black, gothic-style writing.

"If you flash me a smile, you can keep this," the clown whispered, as he leaned in close to Lewis. Was it a whisper? Sounded more like a growl. Was the clown annoyed that Lewis, the one kid he wanted to please, was the one child who didn't seem to appreciate his efforts?

Lewis didn't flash him a smile.

"Lewis.... what do you say to the nice man?"

Lewis looked to me and looked back to the clown, "Fuck you!" he barked.

"LEWIS!"

The other parents took this as their time to leave us to it and, slowly, the crowd dissolved away from us.

"You swore... I swore," he said - a look of complete defiance on his face. I have to confess this was a first and yet I wasn't too angry at him because of who he said it too. He didn't ask the clown to try and put on a show at him. I turned to the clown who simply looked angry.

"I'm so sorry," I said, even though I wasn't actually very sorry at all. He should have minded his own business. The clown simply stood back to his full height... he must have been six foot five... must have heels in those ridiculous shoes. He didn't once take his eyes off Lewis. He smiled again. The huge smile, which showed all of his yellow teeth, made even bigger with the use of the red make-up around his lips - which ended halfway up his painted-white face. With no words, he shrugged and popped the balloon before laughing.

Smile - Matt Shaw

I gave him a puzzled look before taking Lewis' hand and dragging him towards the sports shop. I feel like I should say something to him but... had it been the other way round, I probably would have said the same thing to the clown. He did, after all, butt in where he wasn't invited. I turned to Lewis to see if he, at least, looked sorry for what he said but he wasn't paying any attention. He was simply looking back. I followed his gaze; the clown stood out from the crowd.... watching us walk away - a fixed, crazy grin on his face.

I still hate clowns.

I gave Lewis' hand a sharp tug to make him turn around.

He noticed I was looking at him, "And it was a rubbish balloon...."

He did have a point.

Smile - Matt Shaw

5.

The second sports shop had a better selection of trainers than the first shop we visited but, still, none of them jumped out at me screaming for me to buy them. A lot of them were bright too. I didn't want bright shoes. Not to go to college with. I wanted cool trainers, yes, but... bright... I didn't want to stand out for the wrong reasons.

The prices here are dearer, though. Even with the money I saved on Lewis' shoes I wouldn't have had enough for half of the trainers, on display, here. Typically, the one pair I did really like the look of were more than double what I had left to spend. I wonder if I could ask mum for the extra. They might have paid the difference as part of my birthday next month. I can't do that. I want to finish my driving lessons.... unless, it is an important birthday, maybe they'll do both for me? Would it hurt to ask?

"How much longer?" moaned Lewis, from behind me on the chairs which were meant for people trying on the shoes.

"Ssh!" I hissed.

He huffed and puffed as he fidgeted in his chair. A quick check of my watch showed we were still on track to make it to his precious toy shop as well. Just, as usual, he wanted everything his own way.

I picked up the expensive trainer, a size seven, and caught the eye of one of the shop assistants, "Can I try these on in an eleven, please?"

"Certainly, I'll just see if we have it," said the shop assistant as he took the right footed shoe from me. With that, he disappeared out of the back door - not too far from the wall of trainers.

"I want to go!" shouted Lewis - louder than he had previously shouted since we got to the shopping centre.

"Be quiet! I'm nearly done!" I hissed, looking around to see how many people were looking at us.

"I hate you!" he continued, "I wish I came with mum!"

"And I wish you hadn't been born!" I spat back. I regretted it as soon as the words left my mouth. It was a stupid thing to say - one of those venomous things you spit back when you're angry with someone. A spur of the moment thing...

Lewis jumped off the chair, "I'm going!"

"No, you're not! Sit back down!"

"Fuck you," he shouted - this time loud enough for the whole store to hear. Again, without thinking, I shoved him back against the chairs. Harder than I thought - I just thought he'd have fallen back to a sitting down position, on them, but instead he bounced off and fell to the floor. He stood up - I could see the anger in his eyes.

"I'm going to the toy shop," he shouted again.

I didn't react this time - I felt guilty for how hard I pushed him and the whole shop was watching us. So embarrassing.

"Fine, go... and don't bother coming back!" I shouted back.

Lewis stormed past me and out of the shop. Of course I watched him. He got as far as outside of the store before he stopped and slumped back against the glass window of the shop - making it shake a little from the impact of his weight. If this was Lewis and mum, she would have chased out after him and given into his demands but he needs to know - he needs to know you don't get everything your own way all of the time. I carried on watching him. He must have realised I wasn't coming right out and he slid down the glass until he was sitting on the cold floor of the shopping centre. He'll stay there sulking, I expect. If he really was going off, like he shouted, he wouldn't have stopped.

"We don't have an eleven but we do have a size ten and twelve. I brought them for you to try because sometimes trainers come up a little bigger or a little smaller...." said the shop assistant. I turned to see he did, indeed, have both the size ten and twelve under his arms. Normally shops don't have size twelves - it was typical of my luck that this was the one pair of trainers where the eleven was missing.

"Thank you," I said. "Best to just try the twelves, though... I never fit into tens."

The shop assistant checked which box was which and handed me the size twelve. I opened the box and instantly knew they weren't going to fit me, they looked massive.... couldn't help but think of the clown, outside. They look as though they'd fit him perfectly.

Smile - Matt Shaw

"Not too sure about this," I said. I took the left shoe from the box and pulled the tissues from within the insides, so I could slip my foot in and see exactly how much bigger they were.

"To be honest, most people have said this particular style has come up a little tighter than they were used to wearing.... it could be just a bit too big, in which case we can try an inner-sole or a heel-grip.... You might find one of those will take the extra room up..."

Typical salesman speak, I thought. "We can give it a go," I said.

To be fair to the shop assistant - the shoe wasn't quite as big as I first thought... although, it still didn't fit properly. I was reluctant to try the heel-grip, or inner-sole, as the assistant offered because... well, my feet aren't going to grow anymore and I'd sooner just have shoes that fitted correctly without the need for additional bits and pieces crammed inside. After all, I was going to be wearing these all day for five days a week. They had to be comfortable.

"Are you expecting any more in?" I asked.

The shop-assistant shrugged, "I'm not sure.... we get our deliveries every Wednesday but we don't know what's coming in them until they are actually here... I could try another store for you? We could get them to do a transfer...."

"I'm not sure," I said. "I think I'll carry on looking around and have a think," I said. No point going to all of the effort of transferring them, or even reserving them, from another store because mum still hadn't agreed to funding the difference yet... even loaning me the difference until my next pay day. Besides, I built my hopes up for the trainers now so... you know how it is.... didn't want to go home empty handed.

"Okay, well is there another pair you like the look of?" the assistant asked. I shook my head and thanked him for his time.

There was one more shop, closer to the toy store, I could have a quick look in - from the window of the next shop, they don't appear to have the sort of trainer I like but... maybe they have different styles inside. Certainly can't hurt to look.

I turned to the door and noticed Lewis was no longer slumped against the window, sitting on the floor. A quick look to the other side of the doorway, in case he moved positions... not there either.... can already feel my heart start to pace hard and fast.

I grabbed his pair of shoes, which he had kindly left for me to carry when he stormed out, and headed out of the shop to see if I could see him....

"Lewis?" was there any point in calling his name - so many people milling around, talking amongst themselves... the shopping centre music playing... would he have heard me? "Lewis?!" I called again. Had to try. He might be close enough to hear. Where the hell is he? A quick look around - he's not pacing the front of the shop... he's not looking in any of the other store windows that I can see... he must have gone to the toy store like he said. What a little shit. I never once thought he'd have gone. It looked as though he was staying put. I'm going to kill him.

As quickly as the crowds let me, I ran in the direction of the toy store. It was only around the corner from the shop I was looking in so not too far to run.

As soon as I got there, I hurried across the width of the shop looking down the aisles.... can't see him.

He could be down the other side of the shop, though...

... out of sight....

... I went down the furthest aisle and walked the width again...

... he's not here...

... I can't see him...

... panic setting in now...

"Lewis?" I called out.

He didn't respond.

I feel dizzy.

Where is he?

Where's he wandered off to?

* * * * *

Smile - Matt Shaw

Mum was crying. Tears rolling down her cheeks and she was shaking - just as I had been shaking when I first got to the security office... when I finally realised he was missing. She's pushed me away once. I don't put my arm around her. I don't say anything. What do I say. I've already apologised... I've already told her how sorry I am. I didn't mean for him to run off. I honestly thought he was going to just stay against the glass window of the shop and sulk until I went and got him. I never expected him to run.

"You shouldn't have let him leave the shop!" she said. "You know what he's like.... Where is he? Where?! My baby's lost...."

Thankfully, the door to the security office opened and the guard came back in.

Mum looked up, "Have you found him?"

The man shook his head, "No."

"And the management?"

"The centre's manager has been away for a couple of weeks... annual leave..."

"What about the other security guards?" I asked, trying to be helpful and knowing they had more experience than this man.

He shook his head again.

"What's that supposed to mean?" asked mum.

"I've been calling them on the hand-helds but they aren't answering...."

"So they're missing too?" I asked.

The security guard just looked at me - clearly out of his depth.

"That's it... I'm phoning the police...."

Mum stood up and fished her mobile phone out of the pocket before dialing '999' on the keypad. With the phone ringing, she pressed it against her ear, "Police, please."

I turned to the security guard, "Do your colleagues often wonder off?" I asked. He shook his head again.

Smile - Matt Shaw

"I haven't worked with them before today. Normally it's another guy on, and a lady, that I work with.... Look, they'll show up. They're probably conducting a thorough search for Luke..."

"Lewis..."

"Sorry, Lewis... now... They're probably hunting high and low. The main doors are locked now so if he's in here, they'll find him..."

"If he's in here..." I said.

"Well, Barry said he checked the monitors at the time of the disappearance. He said he didn't see anything."

"Barry?"

"My colleague..."

"Those monitors?" I pointed to the CCTV screens on the desk.

"Yes - he said he checked the store at the time and it just showed Lewis wandering off.... didn't show him being snatched or anything else..."

"I was sat in here from the moment I reported him missing... he didn't check the monitors when I was in here..."

The security guard frowned. "He must have done...."

"I'm telling you...."

"The police are on their way," said mum, interrupting us, as she hung the phone up and slipped it back into her handbag. "What's going on?"

I didn't say anything. Didn't feel as though it was my place to tell her about the missing guards and the fact it looked dubious as to whether they had even done their job properly before they did their amazing vanishing act.

"Just waiting to hear back from my colleagues," said the security officer, keeping his eye on me just in case, I presume, I was to say anything... like the fact they're ignoring his calls.

"The police should have been called immediately!" said mum. "What were you all thinking?"

Smile - Matt Shaw

"I can only apologise," said the guard, "rest assured we're doing everything we can to find him now, though."

"How's that?" I couldn't keep quiet any longer. "You don't even know where your colleagues are, they're ignoring your calls.... and.... it doesn't even look like they checked the monitors.... You said yourself - your colleague told you he had checked them... but I was in here the whole time from reporting Lewis as missing..."

"What's he saying..." said mum.

I ignored her and carried on venting towards the guard who just appeared to be getting smaller and smaller, "... the whole time... not once did he even have a look at the monitors. Not once... by the time I got back from looking around, myself.... you were all in here so you'd have seen him checking the monitors too...."

"Why would he lie to me?" said the security guard.

"You haven't even checked the cameras? My baby is out there somewhere and you haven't even checked to see if you could see what direction he went in.... or whether he was taken...."

Suddenly there was a knock on the security office's door - a loud knock which made us all jump, mum more so than the rest of us.

"Hello?" the security guard called out. He walked over to the door and pulled it open - probably thankful that it had stopped mum and I from hitting him with awkward questions and finger pointing as to the poor job they had been doing. He pulled the door open to reveal two women - both of whom looked visibly shaken. "What can I do for you? The mall is closed now..."

"Our children are missing," said the first of the women - a pretty blonde in her late twenties.

Smile - Matt Shaw

6.

Just as the world outside was probably starting to feel incredibly large, to Lewis, the security office was becoming smaller and increasingly more cramped as the two women stepped inside to explain what had happened to their children. I didn't know what was going on but it was looking less and less likely that Lewis had just wandered off in a sulk. Not with these two women stepping forward to report their children missing too.

"Where did you last see them?" the security guard asked.

"The police are already on their way - my son is missing too," mum said to the ladies. She probably thought she was offering them some comfort but, looking at them, it didn't look as though her words offered much in the way of comfort at all.

"I was at the cash-point getting some money out.... I turned around and she was gone..."

"And I was..." the other lady started.

"You two aren't together?" asked the security guard.

The both shook their heads, "No. I was trying a dress on in Evan's changing room... I came out and he wasn't there... He was on the chairs, by the entrance to the fitting room... he was playing on his Nintendo..." finished the second lady, a larger brunette.

The security guard turned to me, "Look, I know you've told my colleagues already but... if you could tell me again... we'll start from scratch and check the monitors whilst we wait for the police...."

"That's it?" asked the first lady - the pretty blonde in her twenties.

"The police have been called, they're on their way... I can check the screens and see if I can see anything... It's a start," said the security officer. I was watching him closely. Had to be said, he was looking pretty flustered. I bet he wished he hadn't come in today. I know I was wishing the same thing. Should have told mum I was busy. Should have stayed at home. Lewis would still be screaming in his room, kicking off about this or that but... at least we would have known where he was. He turned back to me, "And what shop were you in?"

Smile - Matt Shaw

"Nike," I said. I half expected mum to say something - especially given the standard of shoe I had picked up for Lewis. She didn't say anything. More pressing things on her mind.

"Okay, we'll start with Lewis... and then you," he pointed to the brunette, "and then we'll check for your daughter," he said to the blonde.

We all nodded. There was nothing else we could do, after all. It's not as though we knew how to use the equipment in the office. The security officer turned to me, again, and asked, "Do you know the approximate time?"

"Probably about quarter past four," I said.

"Okay..." he pushed past the brunette lady to get to the screens, "excuse me, please." We all shuffled around to give him the necessary space to get to the desk.

A few buttons were pushed and all the screens flicked to various different images of some of the random stores, within the centre, before it settled on the store-front of Nike. We watched as people walked backwards into and out of the store - as the security guard rewound the tape to the required timeframe, which was displayed in the top right of the monitor's screen.

"About quarter past four...." he confirmed.

I didn't say anything, there was no need, as we saw Lewis come out of the store, on the screen. Pretty much quarter past four on the dot.

"That's my baby," said mum. She broke down into tears. "My baby..." she reached out for the screen but the security guard stopped her.

"We need to see..."

It was strange seeing Lewis throwing his strop from another angle. I watched as he threw himself back against the glass window before sliding down it until he was sat on the floor.

"I watched him do that," I said, "I didn't think he was going to go anywhere... I just thought he was having another tantrum..." I looked at mum, hoping she would have agreed with me in that it didn't look as though he was going anywhere. She didn't say a word. I could see she was fighting back her tears and, if anything, looked a little embarrassed at the, obvious, bad behaviour of her son. Maybe she didn't hear me, "I didn't think he was going anywhere, mum..." I noticed the other two women were looking at me with pity in their eyes. Having lost their own children, they must have known how easy it was to lose them in the crowds. A glance to the security guard and he was still engrossed in the monitors.

"Who's that?" asked the officer.

I looked to the monitor and saw the same clown, from earlier, talking with Lewis.

"Some clown," I said, "he was trying to cheer Lewis up earlier..."

"And you didn't think to say anything?" mum asked.

"I didn't get a chance to say anything, the first time... he told the man to fuck off."

"What?!" mum looked horrified.

"He told him to fuck off and I dragged him away.... we went, from there, to the Nike shop," I said. "I told you..."

"You didn't tell me what he said," said mum. Now she looked really embarrassed.

"He's leaving," the officer said. I turned back to the monitor, avoiding mum's stare and saw the clown leaving Lewis... leaving the shot. "Maybe he was just trying to cheer him up again... he looks pretty upset," the guard finished.

Lewis didn't move, to start with, he just kept sitting there - against the window where I knew he was. A couple more minutes went by, on the monitor, when he suddenly stood up and walked off in the same direction as the clown...

"He's following the man," said mum. "He's following him!" She turned back to me again, "You see what you've done?!"

"The toy shop is in the direction he's walking," I said.

The security officer flicked through various camera angles until he found the store front of the toy shop. He set the time back a bit and we waited.... hoping to see Lewis walk into the store. Approximately six minutes went by before we suddenly saw me run into the shop. I looked at mum and wondered whether she saw how worried I looked. I hope she did. A couple of minutes went by, on the screen, and I came back out again. If only he had been in there.

Smile - Matt Shaw

"Okay, so we aren't sure where he went but at least the tape shows he wandered off by himself..." said the guard.

"What did that man say to him? Maybe he went off to meet him...." asked mum.

"The cameras don't pick up sound," he replied.

The security officer turned to the blonde lady, "Do you remember the approximate time?"

"That's it?" said mum - as though she expected Lewis to suddenly be found.

"You've seen your son just wandered off," said the woman, suddenly getting angry.... "Let me see if my daughter did the same or whether she was snatched..."

Mum ignored the blonde woman and turned back to the security officer, "You must know the company who sent the clown... call them up.... they can get him to give us a ring... let us know what he said... it might help..."

The security guard nodded, "I'll look the company up just as soon as I've checked the other children," he said.

Mum went to say something else but the blonde lady butted in before she could get a word out, "It was the hole in the wall downstairs... next to the gadget shop and toilets."

The guard nodded and flicked through the screens until he found the one of the cash machines next to the gadget shop. It wasn't the best of camera angles but it was better than nothing. "Do you know what time it was?"

The woman shook her head, "Five, I think..."

We all watched as the time counter, in the corner of the screen, whizzed to five o'clock. People, on the screens, coming into and leaving the shot - some with bags of shopping, some stopping to use the cash machines and others disappearing through the doors to the toilet.

"STOP!" shouted the blonde haired lady.

The security guard hit play, slowing the camera's down to normal speed in the process. There, on the screen, we saw her slide her bank card into the cash machine. Behind her, a few feet away, we saw her daughter.

Smile - Matt Shaw

"That's her," she said.

The body language of the little girl, same sort of age as Lewis I would have guessed, was that of someone who was upset. Couldn't tell from her facial expressions, though. The camera footage was too grainy. No one said anything as we continued to watch the little girl - waiting to see what she did next. Like Lewis, did she wander off too or was there someone else involved.

"Is she upset?" asked the brunette lady.

"I had just shouted at her," said the blonde woman. "She wanted to go home but I hadn't finished with what I needed to get done..."

"Look," said the security guard.

The little girl on the screen suddenly turned towards the toilet door. A second or two went by. She looked to her mum and then back to the toilet door.... and then she went through it. The door slammed shut behind her. At not one stage did her mother turn around.

"No, I checked in the toilet... she wasn't in there... it was the first place I checked..." said the lady. True to her word, on the screen she was frantically looking for her daughter. She disappeared into the toilet - out of shot for seconds before she re-appeared without her child.

Just as mum had reacted, the woman started to cry. The other lady, the brunette, put her arm around her. Little comfort for a missing child.

"Can you rewind it to when the girl went into the toilet?" said mum.

The security guard nodded and rewound the recording back to where the girl was looking at the toilet door.

"Can you pause it?" mum asked.

The security guard nodded, "Now?"

"Not yet..."

The girl, on screen, opened the door to the toilet again and mum shouted, "There! Pause it! Look! What is that?"

Both mum and the security guard peered closer to the screen to see what mum had spotted. I didn't need to, though. I knew what she had seen. "It's a bit of a clown's shoe," I said.

Smile - Matt Shaw

"What? What do you mean?" asked the blonde mother - a look of concern on her face.

"The clown who was trying to cheer Lewis up, he was wearing these big red shoes... that looks like it's part of one of the shoes..."

The girl on the screen was even looking up. As though she was looking to someone, in the toilet, who was out of camera shot.

"There wasn't a clown in the toilets though," said the mother. "I went in there... there wasn't a clown.... one locked cubicle...."

"He could have been in the cubicle," I said.

"Then where's my daughter?"

No one wanted to say it but we all knew where she could have been. She could have been locked in the cubicle with Pogo the clown. The security guard un-paused the camera and we waited. First the mother went into the toilet before coming back out.... and then we waited... and waited.... fifteen minutes went by, on the screen, before the door opened again and a tall woman, dragging a suitcase behind her, came out.

"Who's that?" asked the security guard.

No one knew the answer.

"Was the clown a woman?" the security guard turned to me.

"No. Definitely a man."

The security guard hit fast forward again and, again, we watched as people went in and out of the toilet. As the time got closer to when the centre closed, the visitors got less and less. Before long the screen was empty and remained so.

"Where is she?" asked the mother. "Is she still in there?!" No one said anything. "Can you come with me to check?" she asked the security guard.

I stepped forward, "I'll come with you." Anything to get out of the security office. "Is that okay?" I asked the guard. He nodded.

"What about my son?" asked the brunette lady.

Smile - Matt Shaw

"I'll check for him now.... you said you were in a clothes shop?" said the security guard.

I turned to the blonde lady, "Ready?"

She nodded, "Yes please..."

I walked over to mum and gave her a kiss on the cheek, "I'll be back soon..." She didn't react in any way - just kept looking at the screen whilst the security guard hunted for the necessary camera.

Smile - Matt Shaw

7.

"Thank you for coming with me," said the blonde lady.

"No worries, I'm just happy to get out of the office..."

"Have you been in there for long?"

"Since half four, although I did step out to have another look around to see if I could find my brother. I'm Alex, by the way."

"Jackie."

I would have said it was nice to meet her, as we walked down the staff corridor towards the double doors which would lead us to the shopping centre, but... we were only meeting because we had both lost someone close to us. It would have been nicer for us to both be at home, or on the way home at least, having successfully come to town to get the bits we needed before venturing back to our houses. It would have been nicer, still, to be stuck in a traffic jam, outside of the centre... anywhere would have been nicer than here right now.

"Do you think she'll be there?" Jackie said.

I pushed one of the doors open and held it there so she could pass through.

"I'm not sure," I said. I didn't want to give her any false hopes by saying 'yes' - pretending that everything was going to work out okay. I don't think she will still be in the toilet. Why would she be? There's no reason for a child to stay somewhere like that - especially without their parent. Fine - it's possible had they been somewhere like a toy shop, or a playground but... I've never known a child who actively wanted to stay in a public toilet.

I let Jackie lead the way to the restrooms; down the escalators, which had now been switched off - by the other security guards I presumed - and right past a row of different stores, towards the entrance to the shopping centre. I recognised we were in the right place as soon as we got there, from the images I saw on the monitors.

"I'm scared," she said to me. "What if she's not in here?"

I didn't know the right words to offer her any sort of comfort.

Smile - Matt Shaw

Maybe I wasn't the right person to have escorted her.

All this.... all this is new to me.

"What then?" she asked.

I gave her a sympathetic smile. It was all new to me but I knew exactly what she was going through. I had been going through it too and had the same thoughts when I was running around the stores, earlier, trying to find him - both before I went to the security office and after, when I decided it would be worthwhile to have another look for Lewis.

"Did you want me to go in?" I asked.

She nodded.

I was afraid of that.

"What's her name?" I asked. If the girl was in there, stuck in one of the cubicles, she'd be scared. She might feel better if I knew her name, at least. I could reassure her, and tell her that her mum is outside, before coming back out to get Jackie to come in with me.

"Lisa," Jackie replied.

She wiped a tear from her cheek with a shaky hand.

"I'll be right back," I said.

I wonder if the security guard is currently watching us. I hope so. I'd feel a little better if I knew someone else was watching. Was that really the clown's foot we saw on the screen? They didn't come out either. What if the clown is still in here?

I hate clowns.

I think I hate the smiling ones worse.

There's something really sinister about them.

Stephen Fucking King.

I'll never read one of his books again, I swear.

Smile - Matt Shaw

With a shaking hand, I reached out and pushed the door open, before I peered into the room. White tiled floors, white walls, a flowery scent... the scent I didn't expect. Not compared to the smells you normally get in the men's public toilets - a mixture of crap and piss.

We should learn something from the female of the species, I thought, *keep our toilets nice too.*

That's cool, keep thinking things like that.

Keep your mind focused on something other than clowns.

Dammit.

Thinking about clowns again.

"Lisa?" I called out.

No reply came.

Surely, if she were in the room... surely she would have responded. The door slammed shut behind me as I stepped in and I couldn't help but jump. I'm kind of glad there wasn't anyone else around to witness that.

Pathetic.

"Lisa?"

I pushed the first cubicle door open.

Empty.

The second.

Empty.

Third.

Empty.

Two left. She isn't here.

"Lisa, you in here?"

Smile - Matt Shaw

Getting closer to the end of the row of cubicles, and still picturing a clown - with red eyes and a beaming manic grin - jumping out at me, I kicked the fourth cubicle door open with my foot.

Empty.

My heart is beating so fast it feels as though it's going to burst through my chest.

Get a grip.

Sort it out.

Is that sweat I feel dripping down my forehead?

Last door.

"Lisa?"

I kicked the door open and froze when I saw a single red balloon on a piece of string - a weight tied to the other end of the string, holding the balloon a few feet off the floor and stopping it from floating off to the ceiling... 'Smile' written across it... the same type of balloon that was offered to Lewis earlier in the afternoon.

"What is it?" asked Jackie.

I jumped at the sound of her voice, didn't even hear her come in.

"A balloon," I said. I didn't look at her. I couldn't take my eyes off the balloon. I reached into the cubicle and took a hold of the string, pulling the balloon towards me - not even sure why. I didn't want a souvenir from the day.

"Where is she?" said Jackie. Her eyes welled up once more.

I shrugged and put my arms around her.

Unlike my mother she didn't pull away from me and we stood, for a moment, comforting each other. I have to confess, I didn't want the hug to end. For the first time since losing my brother... I felt good. I felt safe. I felt as though everything was okay. When she spoke I felt my world come crashing down around me once more, "Do you think it was the clown?"

I didn't answer her. I didn't know. It was strange finding the balloon here but... it didn't mean anything. Another child could have been given it earlier in the

Smile - Matt Shaw

day. They could have left it in here without thinking. And the clown... was the clown even in here? It looks as though it could have been his foot but... no... I couldn't say for definite. Maybe we just saw what we wanted to see... no... if that were the case, we wouldn't have seen a clown. A shame the security guard couldn't zoom in to get a closer look.

"You aren't answering," she said.

"I don't know," I said. It feels as though that's all I've said today.

"But who else would have taken them?"

"We haven't seen anyone take them," I said - stepping out of our comforting hug. "Lewis wandered off and...."

"... and Lisa just vanished."

"We should get back to the security office. See if anything showed up with the other boy.... and the police might be there. They'll want to speak to us."

Jackie nodded and turned towards the door.

I looked at the balloon.

I don't need to take that.

I was glad to get out of the ladies toilet. The balloon reminded me of the clown. Reminded me of the way he looked at Lewis. Fine, there was no firm evidence he did anything but - he was still a creepy-ass clown.

Jackie and I walked back to the security office in silence. Silence because we'd both run out of things to say to each other or silence because we both hoped we may have heard Lewis or Lisa calling out for us.

"You didn't find her?" the security guard asked.

Jackie shook her head.

"Anything?" I asked mum.

She also shook her head, "The camera didn't show inside the shop.... and...." she looked at the brunette, "couldn't pin point a time she went into the store so we haven't spotted them going in or out..."

Smile - Matt Shaw

I glanced over to the brunette lady. She was just looking at the monitor. Her eyes red-raw. She didn't say anything.

Jackie asked, "Have the police arrived?"

"I've just called them again," my mum said.

Jackie turned to me, "Tell them about the balloon...."

"Balloon?" asked the security guard.

"We found a balloon in the toilet.... the same type that the clown tried to give Lewis.... I mean, it doesn't mean anything... someone else could have taken it into the toilet...."

"But we saw his foot... in the video," said Jackie. She was clutching at anything. The slightest thing to hint at where her daughter was. But then, maybe she was right. Maybe it was his foot in the video.

"He's right," the security guard said as he nodded in my direction, "it doesn't mean he took your daughter.... we didn't see her leave with him... or Lewis... we didn't see him leave with the clown..."

"We should still call the company," said mum. "I want to know what he said to my son!"

"We should wait and let the police investigate this!" said the security guard.

"Nonsense.... find their phone number..... the police will only want it anyway... the clown is a potential witness..." mum continued.

"She's right," I said.

"Fine. We'll call them... as you said, the police will want to talk to them anyway..." The security guard crosses the room over to the other side where there are some filing cabinets against the wall. He pulled open the top drawer of the first cabinet he came to and pulled out a diary. "The name of the company will be in here, under today's date. Should have the phone number...." He flicked through the pages, until he got to today's date, and frowned. "That's strange."

"What is it?" asked Jackie.

"There's no one booked in here..."

Smile - Matt Shaw

"What does that mean?" asked mum.

"It means we shouldn't have had any entertainers walking around.... they shouldn't have been here..." said the guard.

"Maybe they just showed up off the cuff..." I said.

"They wouldn't have been allowed - they would have been asked to leave.... if people come in and want to sell things in the centre, or put on shows or displays... they have to pay a fee.... this clown hasn't paid. He shouldn't have been here..." He closed the diary.

"But you would have seen him on the monitors.... why didn't you ask him to leave?" Jackie was getting angry now. Like my mum, she was working her way through the emotions.

"I don't look at the monitors - I was working in the loading bays for most of the day.... signing in the different deliveries!"

"Then who should have been looking at the screens!" shouted Jackie.

"It was supposed to be my colleague!" said the security guard. Again, I started to feel sorry for him. We were all in the same position. Other than the guard - we had all lost someone. He was only working there but he was coming under fire from all directions.

"And where are they? Where are your colleagues?" asked mum. She too started to raise her voice.

"I don't know!"

"Do you know anything?" asked Jackie. "My daughter...."

"My son," mum chipped in...

"Our children," continued Jackie, "are out there somewhere and you can't even find your fellow work colleagues... what use are you?!"

"Maybe our children are with the security guards.... probably all sat around somewhere having a laugh at our expense!" said mum.

The security guard raised his hands, "Look, this isn't helping... I'm trying my best here. You know I'm new. You know I haven't been at this post today. I was working out the back... I'm not trained for this... I've told you that... the police.... they're on their way... let's just see what they have to say..."

Smile - Matt Shaw

"He's right," I said. I felt as though he needed someone on his side but it just reminded mum I was here.

"You should never have let him out of your sight!" she hissed.

I should have stayed quiet.

"This is your fault," she finished.

"Look, let's all calm down.... we'll look at the screens again, see if we can see anything we may have missed.... until the police come, at least... There's nothing else we can do."

He was right. There was nothing else we could do. There was no point walking around the centre looking around for the missing children or the security guards. Not when the police were on their way. It was best just to stay put. Wait for the police and let them take charge of the situation.

"Can we have another look for my son?" asked the brunette - the only one who hadn't stepped away from the screens. The whole time, since Jackie and I got back from the bathroom, she had sat there - staring at the screen which showed the front of Evans, the store where she lost her son.

"Certainly," said the security guard. He pushed his way back to the desk with the monitors - thankful for the opportunity to get out of the corner where mum and Jackie had backed him.

Jackie glared at him as he stepped around her.

My mother, meanwhile, was just staring at me.

Was that hate in her eyes?

Smile - Matt Shaw

8.

With the tension building in the cramped office - we hadn't noticed the brunette lady was crying again until she was in proper hysterics. Immediately mum and Jackie turned to comfort her, putting aside the fact that their children were also missing. The security guard did his best to ignore the wailing of the lady so as to concentrate on the shop. He had his work cut out for him - not even knowing an approximate time she had originally ventured into the store meant he had to keep his eyes peeled and refrain from blinking. I did my best just to stay out of their way. I'd proven I wasn't the best at comforting people and I was still hurting from the look mum had given me.

I never meant Lewis to run off. I watched him against the window and it looked as though he wasn't going anywhere. Just looked like he was throwing his usual strop. Of course I would have left the store sooner, to run after him, had I noticed him get up and wander off. I would never have let him leave like that. Never. Why wouldn't mum believe me, though? She had looked at me as though it's what I had wanted, right from the start. Like I had planned to lose him as soon as we were away from her. But that's not the case. Lewis and I had been out together on numerous other occasions - always without incident... with the exception of once or twice where tears were concerned but... that's normal when you go out with someone of that age. Especially given his condition.

Will she ever believe me?

If Lewis never comes home...

... will mum realise I didn't do it on purpose?

Will she ever forgive me?

I couldn't live like that - knowing she hated me.

And what will dad say?

Will he think I did it on purpose too?

They have to find him.

They have to.

Smile - Matt Shaw

I'm not leaving.

Not going home.

Not until they find out where he is.

The brunette lady was telling her story through sobs of tears, "I have to find him... we had an argument... I don't want me telling him off being the last thing he heard from my mouth...." she turned to the security guard, ".... please find him...."

The security guard didn't answer but he heard her. His eyes visibly straining as he watched on the monitor for signs of the mother and her son. Part of me just wants to leave the office - carry on wandering around the centre on the off-chance I could see Lewis. Or even Lisa, Jackie's daughter.... or the other lady's son... I felt like a spare part just standing there... towards the back of the room.

"I could go down to the clothes shop?" I offered. I already knew the security guard wouldn't allow it. The shop would be shut now. If the lad was there, the store's staff would have spotted him and phoned through already.

Mum flashed me a look, "You can stay there - the police will be here soon enough."

The police.

Feels like they were phoned ages ago.

I guess three missing children - potentially snatched - aren't high on their list of priorities today. No wonder the police are always under-fire for not doing a good enough job. The police come under-fire first.... and then the government for not offering the police more resources. Same old, same old...

I sat back, on a chair, at the other side of the room and stared at the top row of monitors - unlike the ones the security guard was playing with, these were showing the centre as it was now. With the exception of a few staff members finally being allowed to leave their closed shops - it's near enough empty. If Lewis and the others were here, they would have been found by now. They aren't here. They can't be. I felt my eyes well up.

No.

Give them a wipe.

Smile - Matt Shaw

Don't cry.

Although, if I do... maybe mum will come and comfort me. Maybe she'll see, finally, that I didn't want for this to happen. I just wish I could turn back the clock. Wish I could start the day again.

My mouth reacted quicker than my brain, "Look!" I pointed to the far left screen, across the top row. Dancing his way down the escalators looked to be the same clown who had spoken to Lewis earlier. A load of balloons on strings clutched together in his gloved hand. "That's him!" I don't know why I said that. There hadn't been that many clowns wandering around, after all.

"I've got this," the security guard stood up and leaned in closer to the screen, "that's the first floor...." he turned to us, "okay, wait here for the police - I'll go and have a word with whoever the hell that is..."

I stood up too, "I'm coming with you."

"No, wait here!" the security guard raised his voice.

I stood firm for what felt like the first time, "No, he might remember Lewis if he sees me... I'm coming and you're wasting time. Let's go!"

"I'm coming too," said mum.

The security guard didn't argue anymore as we all quickly filed from the room. He realised there was little point in arguing. The more he argued - the more chance we had of losing the clown.

I never once thought I'd be running through a near-deserted shopping centre, looking for a clown...

The security guard was running at full speed and I struggled to keep up with him. My mother and the other two ladies were left behind but we couldn't wait. They'd catch up with us when we caught up with the clown. We couldn't afford to lose him. Sure, he might not have known anything. What he said to Lewis may have no bearing on what happened to him. It looked as though he had been in the bathroom but - if he had been in there – how had he got out? And the fact he was seen on the screen, clutching a fistful of balloons... well, that just proves he'd been giving them out all day - even if he didn't have permission to be there.

I nearly stumbled as we ran down the escalators. I always struggled with keeping my balance on escalators after they'd been turned off. Like my brain struggled to cope with making sense of them because of the lines on each step... you look down at them, when they're stationary, and they don't resemble stairs... instead, they just look as though they're a slope. Copying the security guard I jumped down the last few stairs.

"You! Wait there! I need a word!" the security guard called out.

There, in the distance, about to disappear down the stairs towards the car-park was the clown.

"FREEZE!" the security guard shouted again.

The clown froze - over exaggerating his movements - mid-step.... one leg high in the air, the other leg at a funny angle... one arm, with the hand still clutching the balloons, stretched far in front of him and the other arm stretched out behind him. A manic grin on his face.

It wasn't long before we were stood next to him.

He didn't look at us.

He just kept staring dead ahead as though he were literally frozen to the spot.

"Who are you?" asked the security guard.

The clown mumbled through his over-stretched smile, "Can I unfreeze?" He didn't wait for an answer, he simply stood up straight and slowly turned to look at the security guard. His grin remained fixed in place.

"Funny, you can stop smiling too...." said the security guard - obviously put off by it. I couldn't say I blamed him. It wasn't the nicest of smiles.

"If only I could...." growled the clown in his deep voice, "... industrial accident.... acid.... the smile stays.... but trust me.... I'm crying on the inside..."

I looked at the security guard. He simply looked nervous.

The clown laughed, a high-pitched squeal of a laugh which didn't suit his outward appearance, "Not really..." he stopped smiling and, for the first time since I'd originally seen him, looked semi-human. "I just prefer it." He smiled once more and fixed it in place. "Smile and the world smiles with you... a smile brightens up the day for you and those around you.... don't you think?!"

"Can you just be serious for a minute..."

Smile - Matt Shaw

"Give it a go," he hissed.

"Some children have gone missing today...."

The clown did an over-exaggerated 'shocked' face. "Oh no!" He stopped when he realised the security guard wasn't laughing.

"I need you to come with me. Give a statement to the police..."

I butted in, "It was my brother... the one who swore at you..."

The clown adopted a serious voice, "I remember him. Short. Needs to smile more."

I continued, "He's gone missing."

Another 'shocked' expression.

Again I ignored it, "And you were the last person to talk to him..."

Mum, Jackie and the other lady showed up behind us. The clown gave them a look and then turned back to me.

"I've spoken to lots of children today. I kind of attract them.... I mean, I am a clown...."

"What were you doing here? You shouldn't have been here...." the security guard interrupted.

"What?"

"We didn't have any entertainment booked in."

"What did you say to my boy?" mum said from the back of the group. The clown leaned around the security guard and I to see who was addressing him this time.

"I can't quite recall... spoken to so many children...."

"My daughter?"

The clown shrugged, "Maybe." He looked back to my mother, "Your son has a potty mouth...."

"Fuck you!" screamed mum.

Smile - Matt Shaw

The clown looked at me. Another over-exaggerated expression of shock. "I guess we know where he gets it from."

The security guard addressed everyone, "Look, can you let me do my job please..." He turned to the clown, "You shouldn't have been here. You didn't have permission. What were you doing..."

"Every week, my troupe and I travel the country and visit places such as this..." he said, a serious voice for the first time since speaking to us, "...put on little shows for the children who don't look as though they're having any fun. We just want to spread a few smiles to the miserable. Spread some joy. Make children smile." He flashed us his smile again before turning to Jackie, "So.... if your daughter was miserable... I may have spoken to her. I may have even given her a balloon...." He turned to the security guard, "If I should have had permission, I apologise..." He looked to mum, "And if your son told me to fuck off.... you should have washed his mouth out with soap!" Another flash of his smile.

"Look, you're a potential witness... you're going to have to come with us and have a chat with the police. You were the last seen to be speaking to this lady's son..."

"He's missing. How do you know he isn't talking to someone right now... and if that is the case... surely the person he is talking to... right now.... surely they are the last person he is speaking too...."

The security guard looked flummoxed.

"...Besides....." continued the clown, "I have a party I need to get to and my friends are waiting for me in the car park... I have a card in there - I'll be only too happy to pass one to you..."

The security guard didn't know what to say. Neither did anyone else. Whatever we said, the clown had an answer... and, if he did have the children... he doesn't have them now. The guard nodded. The clown copied his nod and about turned - continuing his way down the stairs towards the car-park.

Smile - Matt Shaw

9.

The car-park was near enough empty now. Just a few cars and, against the far wall, a van which was covered in paintings of clowns. It didn't take a genius to figure out which was the vehicle we were heading for.

As we made our way closer to the van, the engine spat into life and the lights came on - helping to illuminate the otherwise dimly-lit space. I couldn't make out the driver but he drove the van towards us - to save the wear and tear on our shoes or because he couldn't be bothered to wait for us to get to him, I'm not sure.

When the van was next to us - the driver wound down the tinted window, another clown. I still hate clowns.

He turned to 'our' clown, "You know - I'm not sure we're going to have room for everyone.... did you have a favourite?"

'Our' clown didn't say anything. He simply walked around to the passenger side, opened the door, and jumped in. The security guard walked around, with him. "Did you have a card then?" He had barely finished the sentence when the clown produced a business card from the glove compartment. I was a little disappointed when a springy-snake thing didn't shoot out of the glove-box after the clown opened it. "Thank you. Mind if I take a look in the back of the van?"

"Knock yourself out..." said the driver - a far more serious looking clown than the one we were used to dealing with. No manic smile here. More of a stern look.

I followed the security guard around to the back of the van and heard the door-lock click open. He gave me a slightly uneasy look and whispered to me, "I hate clowns." I couldn't help but smile.

A nice tension breaker.

The guard took a hold of the handle and pulled the door open to reveal another four clowns - all in full make-up. Sat on the floor of the otherwise empty-van. All pulling silly faces and waving at us. One of the most surreal things I'd ever seen, yes.... but no children.... and no traces of any children. The guard smiled back and slammed the door shut.

Smile - Matt Shaw

We walked back to the front of the van. Mum was looking at us - a look of 'hope' on her face. I shook my head.

"My friend here says you're missing some children...." said the driver - a stern look still on his face. "You know... children who wander off.... they're never missing... you're just not looking in the right places... You check the ice-cream shops.... you check the toy shops... you check the playgrounds.... you look properly, you always find them eventually. Anyway, I hope you find them... really, I do... maybe we could come and do a party for them sometime...." There was something in his insincere tone which must have annoyed the security guard as much as me.

"Do you guys ever take your make-up off?" the guard asked.

The driver simply leaned out of the window, closer to the guard, and whispered, "What make-up?"

The passenger flashed us another of his manic grins and the van wheel-span from the car-park.... just as a police car pulled in.

Jackie turned to the security guard, "We haven't checked the play area. Did anyone check it?"

I looked at the security guard, "There's a play area here?"

He nodded, "A soft play area just through there..." he pointed through some double doors. A sign stating the play area was on the other side. All this time, I'd never known there was a play area.

"How come we didn't see video from that in the security office?" I asked.

"They have their own CCTV system - monitored by the staff... but it closed at half four.. The staff would have told us if they had any children there who hadn't been collected..." He turned towards the police car as it pulled to a stop close by. "Excuse me a minute," he said walking off.

I turned to the double doors - a strange uneasy feeling creeping over me... maybe left over from the sight of all those clowns. Maybe something else. I turned to mum and she too was looking at the double doors.

"Shall I?"

She nodded.

Smile - Matt Shaw

I led the way closely followed by Jackie, mum and the other lady - through the double doors and down a short corridor towards another set of double doors with tinted windows... signs on the door 'KidZone'. I pushed the door but they didn't want to seem to budge. It was as though something was blocking them. A harder budge and they moved a fraction more. They weren't locked. Something was definitely blocking them or keeping them back. Using my whole body-weight, I threw myself against the door and it swung open.... something clicking on when the door was fully open.... music began to play but no lights flickered on.... pitch black.

"What's that?" I asked.

"Louis Armstrong?" said mum.

When you're smiling ... when you're smiling..... the whole world... smiles.... with you...... played the song.

"Who's there?" I called out. I could see something in the darkness. Shapes. Looked like people.

"I think I've found the light," said the brunette.

Click.

Keep on smiling..... and the whole world.... smiles.... with you........

The lights flickered on and the room burst into light. Mum screamed, followed by Jackie... my eyes adjusted to the sudden light. On the floor, in front of me, were the two security guards - their eyes ripped from their sockets and throats pulled out....

Don't be sick.

Don't scream.

Be strong...

I turned to mum... I thought she and Jackie had screamed at the sight of the guards but they hadn't.... they had rushed deeper into the room.... past a load of balloons..... I ran to their side.... Oh God...

No...

I started to cry.

Smile - Matt Shaw

All of us were crying.

The door swung open again and the security guard came in with two police officers. They too looked shocked.

We had found Lewis, Lisa and the other boy... slumped against the soft wall of the play area... their faces...

Oh God...

The record had stopped. All I could hear was my own heart-beat and the sobbing of the women.... the police calling for back up.... the security guard saying he had found two more bodies in the back area - those of the staff... All I could see... All I could see was Lewis' face... His cheeks sliced upwards, from the corner of his mouth - the shape of a massive smile.... his mouth and the fresh cuts... stitched shut into a freakish smile....

"Jesus Fucking Christ!" shouted the security guard when he noticed the faces of the children. He crouched down next to Lewis... he's breathing... He's alive...

The police officers felt for a pulse on the other children, they too were breathing. They were alive. All the children lived.

But what happens when they wake up?

The clown's voice played over the speaker system - pre-recorded on the end of the song, "We just want to spread a few smiles to the miserable. Spread some joy. Make children smile."

"Shut that thing off!" one of the police officers shouted.

~ FIN

Smile - Matt Shaw

LIKED WHAT YOU'VE READ?

WHY NOT HEAD OVER TO FACEBOOK
AND CHECK OUT MATT SHAW'S AUTHOR PAGE?

THE ONLY PLACE TO READ SNIPPETS OF NEW WORK AND GET ALL THE LATEST NEWS ON FREE BOOKS AND DOWNLOADS FROM THE DARK WORLD OF MATT SHAW.

LIKE THE PAGE TODAY AND GET A FREE BOOK, FROM MATT SHAW, EMAILED DIRECTLY TO YOU!

TO GET YOUR FREE BOOK - LIKE THE PAGE AND THEN EMAIL
MATT@MATTSHAWPUBLICATIONS.CO.UK

Smile - Matt Shaw

Printed in Great Britain
by Amazon.co.uk, Ltd.,
Marston Gate.